The Adventures of Bob White

The Adventures of Bob White

By THORNTON W. BURGESS

Illustrated by HARRISON CADY

ÆONIAN PRESS

MATTITUCK

To the Reader

It is our pleasure to keep available uncommon fiction and to this end, at the time of publication, we have used the best available sources. To aid catalogers and collectors, this title is printed in an edition limited to 300 copies.—— Enjoy!

ISBN 0-88411-776-6

AEONIAN PRESS, INC.
Box 1200
Mattituck, New York 11952

Manufactured in the United States of America

Contents

CONTENTS

Illustrations

ILLUSTRATIONS

The Adventures of Bob White

He has become fond of Old Mr. Toad

I

A Cheerful Worker

A cheery whistle or a song
Will help the daily work along.

THE little feathered people of the Green Meadows, the Green Forest, and the Old Orchard learned this long ago, and it is one reason why you will so often find them singing with all their might when they are hard at work building their homes in the spring. Most of them sing, but there is one who whistles, and it is such a clear and cheery whistle that it gladdens the hearts of all who hear it. Many and many a time has Farmer Brown's boy stopped to whistle back, and never has he failed to get a response.

A handsome little fellow is this whistler. He is dressed in brown, white, and black, and his name is Bob White. Sometimes he is called a Quail and sometimes a Partridge, but if you should ask him he would tell you promptly and clearly that he is Bob White, and he answers to no other name. All the other little people know and love him well, most of them for the cheery sound of his whistle; but a few, like Reddy Fox and Redtail the Hawk, for the good meal he will make them if only they are smart enough to catch him.

Farmer Brown's boy loves him, not only for his cheerful whistle, but because he has found out that Bob White is a worker as well as a whistler, one of the best workers and greatest helpers on the farm. You see, a part of the work of Farmer Brown's boy is to keep down the weeds and destroy the insects that eat up the crops. Now weeds spring up from seeds. If there were no weed seeds there would be no weeds. In the same way, if there were no insect eggs there would be no insects. But there are millions and millions of both, and so all summer long Farmer Brown's boy has to fight the weeds and the insects. He is very thankful for any help he may get, and this is one reason he has become so fond of Old Mr. Toad, who helps him keep the garden clear of worms and bugs, and of Tommy Tit the Chickadee and others of the little feathered people who live in the Old Orchard and hunt bugs among the apple trees. You know the surest way of winning friends is to help others.

Bob White not only catches worms and bugs, but eats the seeds of weeds, scratching them out where they have hidden in the ground, and filling his little crop with them until he just has to fly to the nearest fence and tell all the world how happy he is to be alive and have a part in the work of the Great World. Not one of all the little people is of greater help to Farmer Brown's boy than Bob White. All the long day he works, and with him works Mrs. Bob and all the little Bobs, scratching up weed seeds here, picking off bugs there, all the time so happy and cheerful that everybody in the neighborhood is happy and cheerful too. The best of it is, Bob White is always just that way. You would think he never had a thing in the world to worry about. But he does have. Yes, indeed! Bob White has plenty to worry about, as you shall hear, but he never allows his troubles to interfere with his cheerfulness if he can help it.

"Bob White! Bob White!" with all his might
He whistles loud and clear.
Because no shame e'er hurt his name
He wants that all shall hear.

One day Peter Rabbit sat listening to it, and it reminded him that he hadn't called on Bob White for some time, and also that there were some things about Bob White that he didn't know. He decided that he would go at once to call on Bob and try to satisfy his curiosity. So off he started, lipperty-lipperty-lip.

II

Bob White Has Visitors

"Bob White! Bob White! I bid the world good cheer!
Bob White! Bob White! I whistle loud and clear!"

THAT very same morning Bob White had taken it into his head to come over to live not very far from the dear Old Briar-patch where Peter Rabbit lives. Of course,

Peter didn't know that Bob had come over there to live. For that matter, I doubt if Bob White knew it himself. He just happened over that way and liked it, and so finally he made up his mind to look about there for a place to make his home.

Now Peter Rabbit had known Bob White for a long time. Peter, in his roaming about, had met Bob a number of times, and they had passed the time of day. Whenever Peter had heard Bob whistling within a reasonable distance he had made it a point to call on him. Bob is such a cheery fellow that somehow Peter always felt better for just a word or two with him. So when Bob began to whistle that spring morning Peter hurried over, lipperty-lipperty-lip, to call. He didn't have far to go, for Bob was sitting on a fence post just a little way from the dear Old Briar-patch.

"Good morning," said Peter. "You seem to be very cheerful this morning."

"Why not?" replied Bob White. "I'm always cheerful. It's the only way to get along in this world."

"It must be that you don't have much to worry about," retorted Peter. "Now if you had to run for your life as often as I have to, perhaps you wouldn't find it so easy to be always cheerful."

Bob White's bright little eyes twinkled. "The trouble with a lot of people is that they think that no one has worries but themselves," said he. "Now there is Reddy Fox coming this way. What do you suppose he is coming for?"

"For me!" exclaimed Peter promptly, preparing to scamper back to the Old Briar-patch.

"Nothing of the kind," replied Bob White. "Don't think you are so important, Peter. He doesn't know you are over here at all. He has heard me whistling, and he's coming to see if he can't give me a little surprise. It's me and not you he is after. What's your hurry, Peter?"

"I — I think I'd better be going; I'll call again when you haven't other visitors," shouted Peter over his shoulder.

Hardly had Peter reached the dear Old Briar-patch when Reddy Fox reached the fence where Bob White was sitting. "Good morning," said he, trying to make his voice sound as pleasant as he could. "I'm glad to see you over here. I heard you whistling and hurried over here to welcome you. I hope you will like it here so well that you will make your home here."

"That is very nice of you," replied Bob White, his eyes twinkling more than ever, for he knew why Reddy hoped he would make his home there. He knew that Reddy hoped to find that home and make a good dinner on Quail some day. "It is very pleasant over here, and I don't know but I will stay. Everybody seems very neighborly. Peter Rabbit has just called."

Reddy looked about him in a very sly way but with a hungry look in his eyes as he said, "Peter always is neighborly. Is he anywhere about now? I should like to pay my respects to him."

"No," replied Bob White. "Peter

"Here comes Old Man Coyote!"

left in something of a hurry. Hello! Here comes Old Man Coyote. People certainly *are* neighborly here. Why, what's your hurry, Reddy?"

"I have some important matters to attend to over in the Green Forest," replied Reddy, with a hasty glance in the direction of Old Man Coyote. "I hope I'll see you often, Bob White."

"I hope so," replied Bob White politely, and then added under his breath, "but I hope I see you first."

III

Bob Decides to Build a Home

OLD Man Coyote's call was very much like that of Reddy Fox. He was very, very pleasant and told Bob White that he was very glad indeed that Bob had come over on the Green Meadows, and he hoped that he would stay. No one could have been more polite than was Old

Man Coyote. Bob White was just as polite, but he wasn't fooled. No, indeed. He knew that, just like Reddy Fox, the reason Old Man Coyote was so glad to see him was because he hoped to catch him some fine day. But Bob White didn't let a little thing like that bother him. Ever since he could remember he had been hunted. That was why he had taken the precaution to sit on a fence post when he whistled. Up there neither Old Man Coyote nor Reddy Fox could reach him. Just after Old Man Coyote left, Bob White saw someone else headed his way, and this time he didn't wait.

You see, it was Redtail the Hawk, and a fence post was no place to receive a call from him.

Spreading his wings, Bob White flew across to the dear Old Briar-patch and dropped in among the brambles close to where Peter Rabbit was sitting. "You didn't expect me to return your call so soon, did you, Peter?" said he.

"No," replied Peter, "but I'm ever so glad to see you just the same. Did you have a pleasant call from Reddy Fox?"

"Very," replied Bob White with a chuckle. "He was ever so glad to see me. So was Old Man Coyote. I didn't wait to see what Old Redtail would say, but I have a feeling that he would have liked better to have seen me a little nearer. You see, Peter, you are not the only one who has to keep his eyes open and his wits about him all the time. There are just as many looking for me as for you, but I don't allow that to make me any the less cheerful. Every time I whistle I know that someone is going to come looking for me, but I whistle just the same. I just have to, because in spite of all its troubles life is worth living and full of happiness. Now I've got a secret to tell you."

"What is it?" asked Peter eagerly.

"Promise not to tell a single soul," commanded Bob White.

"Can't I tell Mrs. Peter? I never keep secrets from her, you know," replied Peter.

"Well, you may tell her, but she must promise to keep it secret," said Bob.

"I'll promise for her and for myself," declared Peter. "What is it?"

"I've decided to come over here to live," replied Bob White.

"Right here in the Old Briar-patch?" asked Peter excitedly.

"No, but not far from here," replied Bob White. "I'm going back to the Old Pasture after Mrs. Bob, and we are going to build a home right away."

"Goody!" cried Peter, clapping his hands. "Where are you going to build?"

"That," replied Bob White, "is for Mrs. Bob to decide."

"And when she does you'll tell me where it is so that I can come over and call, won't you?" cried Peter.

"That depends," replied Bob White. "You know there are some things it is better not to know."

"No, I don't know," retorted Peter. "I'm your friend, and I don't see what harm it could do for me to know where your home is."

"Without meaning to, friends sometimes do the most harm of anyone, especially if they talk too much," replied Bob White. "Now the way is clear and I must hurry back to the Old Pasture to tell Mrs. Bob how nice it is here." And with this away he flew.

"Now what did he mean by friends who talk too much," muttered Peter. "Could he have meant me?"

IV

Bob White and Peter Become Neighbors

Who strictly minds his own affairs
And cheerfully doth labor,
He is the one whom I would choose
Always to be my neighbor.

THAT is just the kind of a neighbor Peter Rabbit found Bob White to be. Bob and Mrs. Bob had come down from the Old Pasture and built their home near the dear Old Briar-patch and so had become the neighbors of Peter and little Mrs. Peter. Bob was very neighborly. He often dropped in to have a chat with Peter, and Peter was always glad to see him, for he is such a cheerful fellow that Peter always felt better for having him about. It always is that way with cheerful people. They are just like sunshine.

But though Bob and Mrs. Bob had built their home near Peter, he didn't know just where it was. No, Sir, Peter didn't know just where that home of the Bob Whites was. It wasn't because he didn't try to find

Bob was very neighborly

out. Oh, my, no! Peter could no more have helped trying to find out than he could have helped breathing. That was the curiosity in him. He wasted a great deal of time trying to find Bob White's home, all to no purpose. At first he was rather put out because Bob White wouldn't tell him where it was hidden. But Bob just smiled and told Peter that the reason he wouldn't was because he thought a great deal of Peter and wanted him for a friend always.

"Then," said Peter, "I should think you would tell me where your home is. There ought not to be secrets between friends. I don't think much of a friendship that cannot be trusted."

"How would you feel, Peter, if harm came to me and my family through you?" asked Bob White.

"Dreadfully," declared Peter. "But do you suppose I would let any harm come to you? A nice kind of a friend you must think me!"

"No," replied Bob White soberly, "I don't think you would let any harm come to us if you knew it. But you've lived long enough, Peter, to know that there are eyes and ears and noses watching, listening, smelling everywhere all the time. Now supposing that when you were sure that nobody saw you, somebody *did* see you visit my house. Or supposing Reddy Fox just happened to run across your tracks and followed them to my house. It wouldn't be your fault if something dreadful happened to us, yet you would be the cause of it. You remember what I told you the other day, that there are some things it is better not to know."

Peter looked very thoughtful and pulled his whiskers while he turned this over in his mind. "That is a new idea to me," said he at last. "I never had thought of it before. I certainly never would be able to forgive myself if anything happened to you because of me."

"Of course you wouldn't," replied Bob White. "No more would I ever be able to forgive myself if anything happened to my family because I had told someone where my home is."

Peter nodded. "Of course if I should just happen to *find* your home all by myself, you wouldn't be angry, would you?" he asked.

Bob White laughed. "Of course not," said he. "Just the same I would advise you not to *try* to find it. Then you will have nothing to trouble your mind if you should be followed and something dreadful did happen to me or mine. You see, there are just as many who would like to make a dinner of me as there are who would like to make a dinner of you, and I would a whole lot rather sit on a fence post and whistle than to fill somebody's stomach."

"And I would a lot rather have you," declared Peter.

V

Others Are Interested in Bob White

PETER RABBIT wasn't the only one who was interested in Bob White and in Bob's hidden home. Oh, my, no! It seemed to Peter that Reddy and Granny Fox were prowling around the dear Old Briar-patch most of the time. At first he didn't understand it. "It isn't me they are after, because they know well enough that they can't catch me here," said he to himself, as he watched them one morning. "It isn't Danny Meadow Mouse, because Danny hasn't been over this way for a long time. I don't see how it can be Bob White, because he isn't likely to stay on the ground while they are around, and they can't catch him unless he is on the ground."

He was so busy trying to puzzle out what should bring Reddy and Granny that way so often that he neither saw nor heard Jimmy Skunk steal up behind him.

"Boo!" said Jimmy

"Boo!" said Jimmy, and Peter nearly jumped out of his skin.

"What did you do that for?" demanded Peter indignantly.

"Just to teach you that you shouldn't go to sleep without keeping your ears open," replied Jimmy with a grin.

"I wasn't asleep!" protested Peter crossly. "I was just watching Reddy and Granny Fox and wondering what brings them over here so much."

"You might just as well have been asleep," replied Jimmy. "Supposing I had been my cousin, Shadow the Weasel."

Peter shivered at the very

thought. Jimmy continued: "You are old enough to know, Peter, that it isn't safe to be so interested in one thing that you forget to watch out for other things. As for Reddy and Granny Fox, you ought to know what brings them over this way so much."

"What?" demanded Peter.

"Hasn't Bob White got a nest somewhere around here?" asked Jimmy by way of answer.

"Y-e-s," replied Peter slowly, "I suppose he has. But what of that?"

"Why, Reddy and Granny are looking for it, stupid," replied Jimmy.

Peter stared at Jimmy a minute in

a puzzled way. "What do they want of that?" he asked finally. "They don't eat eggs, do they?"

"Eggs hatch out into little birds, don't they?" demanded Jimmy. "If Reddy and Granny can find that nest, they'll wait until the eggs have hatched into birds and then, well, I've heard say that there is nothing more delicious than young Quail. Now do you see?"

Peter did. Of course he did. He understood perfectly. Reddy and Granny had heard Bob White whistling over there every day; they knew that meant his home wasn't far away. It was all very plain now.

"By the way, you don't happen to know where that nest is, do you?" asked Jimmy carelessly.

"No, I don't!" exclaimed Peter, and suddenly was glad that he didn't know about that nest. "What do you want to know for?" he demanded suspiciously.

"I'm hungry for some eggs," confessed Jimmy frankly.

"You wouldn't rob Mr. and Mrs. Bob White of their eggs, would you?" cried Peter. "I thought better of you than that, Jimmy Skunk."

Jimmy grinned. "Don't get excited, Peter," said he. "I'm told that Mrs. Bob lays a great many eggs, and if that's the case, she wouldn't miss a few."

"Jimmy Skunk, you're horrid, so there!" declared Peter.

"Don't blame me," retorted Jimmy. "Old Mother Nature gave me a taste for eggs, just as she gave Reddy Fox a taste for Rabbit. You haven't any idea where that nest is, have you?"

"No, I haven't! If I had, I wouldn't tell you," declared Peter.

"Well, so long," replied Jimmy good-naturedly. "I think I'll have a look for it. I don't wish Bob White and his wife the least bit of harm, but I would like two or three of those eggs." And with this Jimmy Skunk ambled out to look for Bob White's nest.

VI

The Cunning of Mr. and Mrs. Bob White

WHEN Bob White brought Mrs. Bob down to the Green Meadows from the Old Pasture in the beautiful springtime, she was as delighted as he had hoped she would be. Very wisely he had not even hinted that he thought there was the place of all places for them to build their home. He knew that she would never be satisfied unless she felt that she was the one who had chosen the place for their home. So Bob didn't so much as hint that he had a home in mind. He didn't even tell her how beautiful it was over on the Green Meadows near the dear Old Briar-patch. He let her find it out for herself.

Now little Mrs. Bob was very anxious to get to housekeeping, and no sooner did she reach the Green Meadows than she made up her mind that here was the place of all places for a home. In the first place it was very beautiful, and Mrs. Bob has an eye for beauty. In the second place there was plenty to eat, one of the most important things to consider when you are likely to have a great many little mouths to feed. In the third place there were plenty of good hiding places, and lastly, Mrs. Bob liked the neighbors.

Bob White took care not to let her see that he was tickled. He gravely pointed out to her the fact that Granny and Reddy Fox, Old Man Coyote, and Redtail the Hawk would soon discover that they were living there, and then there would be danger all the time and they would never know what it was to be free from worry.

"Not a bit more than in the Old Pasture where we built last year," snapped Mrs. Bob. "You know as well as I do that wherever we build we will be in danger. It always has been so, and I guess it always will be so. We've been smart enough to fool our enemies before, and I guess we can do it again. I'm not afraid even if you are."

Bob hastened to say that he wasn't afraid. He wouldn't have her think that for the world. Oh, my, no! He was just pointing out the dangers so that they might make no mistake.

Mrs. Bob didn't half hear what he was saying. She was too busy poking about, running here, running there, and all the time using her sharp little eyes for all they were worth. Bob waited patiently, a twinkle in his own eyes. He knew that when Mrs. Bob made up her mind that was all there was to it. Presently she called to him in a low voice, and he flew over to join her.

"Here," she announced, "is where we will build."

Bob looked the ground over with a critical eye. "Don't you think, my dear, that this is rather close to the Crooked Little Path?" he asked. "I have noticed that Reddy Fox and Jimmy Skunk use this path a great deal, not to mention Farmer Brown's boy."

"That's what makes it the safest place on the Green Meadows, stupid," declared little Mrs. Bob. "They will never think to look for our home so close to where they pass. These weeds are very thick and will hide our nest completely. This old fallen fence post will give splendid protection on one side. The Old Briar-patch is so near that in case of need we can get to it in a hurry and there be perfectly safe. You mark my words, Bob White, no one will think of looking here for our nest if you use your common sense and do all your whistling far enough away. Reddy and the others are going to do all their hunting around the place you do your whistling, so it is for you to make this the very safest place in the world. Do you see?"

"Yes, my dear," replied Bob meekly. "You are very clever and cunning. I never should have thought of choosing such a place, but I guess you are quite right."

"I know I am," retorted Mrs. Bob. "Now you fly over to the other side of the Old Briar-patch and whistle while I get busy here. I am anxious to get to work at once."

Bob looked at his little brown wife with admiration. Then he discreetly ran under cover of the weeds and grass until he thought it was safe to take wing, after which he flew to the other side of the dear Old Briar-patch and there began to whistle as only he can.

VII

Bob White Finds That Mrs. Bob Is Right

A quarrel you may often stay
By letting others have their way.

AND you will find, too, that other people are quite as likely to be right as you are. Now while Bob White told Mrs. Bob that he guessed she was right in choosing the place she did for their home, he was not at all sure of it in his own mind. It wasn't a place he would have chosen if the matter had been left to him. No, Sir, that place wouldn't have been his choice. He knew of at least half a dozen places which he thought much better and safer. But, after all, this was to be Mrs. Bob's home even more than his, for she was the one who would have to stay there all the long days sitting on those beautiful white eggs they hoped to have soon.

So Bob kept his opinions to himself, and if he worried a little because the new home was so close to the Crooked Little Path along which Reddy and Granny Fox went so often, he said nothing and brought his share of grasses, straw, and leaves with which to build the nest. Mrs. Bob was very particular about that nest. Just a common open nest wouldn't do. Perhaps in that wise little head of hers she guessed just what was going on in Bob's mind and how he really didn't approve at all of building there. So she made a very clever little roof or dome of grasses and straw over the nest with a little entrance on one side. When it was all done only the very sharpest eyes ever would discover it.

Of course Bob was proud of it, very proud indeed. "My dear, it's the finest nest I've ever seen," he declared. "I hope, I do hope no one will find it."

Mrs. Bob looked at him sharply. "Why don't you own up that you wish it was somewhere else?" she demanded.

Bob looked a little foolish. "I can't quite get over the idea that this is a very dangerous place," he confessed. "But I've great faith in your judgment, my dear," he hastened to add.

"Then see to it that you are careful when you come over this way and never under any circumstances fly directly here," retorted Mrs. Bob. "Keep away unless I call for you, and when you do come, fly over in the long grass back there and then keep out of sight and walk over here under cover of the grass and weeds."

Bob promised he would do just as she had told him to, and to prove it he stole away through the long grass and did not take wing until he was far from the nest. Then he flew over beyond the dear Old Briar-patch and whistled with all his might from sheer happiness.

It wasn't long before there were fifteen beautiful white eggs in the nest in the weeds beside the

Crooked Little Path, and then Bob's anxiety increased, you may be sure. Time and time again he saw Reddy Fox or Granny Fox or Jimmy Skunk trot down the Crooked Little Path, and he knew that they were coming to look for his nest. But never once did they think of looking in that patch of weeds, for it never entered their heads that anyone would build so close to a path they used so much. But they hunted and hunted everywhere else.

And all the time little Mrs. Bob sat on those white eggs and the color of her cloak was so nearly the color of the brown grasses and leaves that

*He saw Granny Fox trot down
the Crooked Little Path*

even if they had looked straight at her it isn't at all likely that they would have seen her. Little by little Bob confessed to himself that Mrs. Bob was right. She had chosen the very safest place on the Green Meadows for their home. It was safest because it was the last place anyone would look for it. Then Bob grew less anxious and spent all his spare time in fooling those who were looking for his home.

VIII

Bob Fools His Neighbors

"All's fair in love and war," 'tis said.
Of course, this isn't true.
A lot is done that's most unfair
And no one ought to do.

IT is always so when hate rules, and the queer thing is it is also true sometimes when love rules. Love quite often does unfair things and then tries to excuse them. But

Bob White didn't feel that there was anything unfair in trying to fool his neighbors. Not a bit of it. You see, he was doing it for love and war both. He was doing it for love of shy little Mrs. Bob and their home, and for the kind of war that is always going on in the Green Forest and the Green Meadows. Of course, the little people who live there don't call it war, but you know how it is—the big people all the time trying to catch those smaller than themselves, and the little people all the time trying to get the best of the big people.

So Bob White felt that it was

perfectly fair and right that he should fool those of his neighbors who were hunting for his home, and so it was. He would sit on a fence post whistling as only he can whistle, and telling all the world that he, Bob White, was there. Presently he would see Reddy Fox trotting down the Crooked Little Path and pretending that he was just out for a stroll and not at all interested in Bob or his affairs. Then Bob would pretend to look all around as if to see that no danger was near. After that he would fly over to a certain place which looked to be just the kind of a place for a nest, and there he would hide in the grass.

Just as soon as he disappeared, Reddy Fox would grin in that sly way of his and say to himself, "So that's where your nest is! I think I'll have a look over there."

Then he would steal over to where he had seen Bob disappear, and poke his sharp nose into every bunch of grass and peek under every little bush. Bob would wait until he heard those soft footsteps very near him, then he would fly up with a great noise of his swift little wings as if he were terribly frightened, and from a distant fence post he would call in the most anxious-sounding voice. Reddy would be sure then that he was near the nest and would hunt and hunt. All the time little Mrs. Bob would be sitting comfortably on those precious eggs in the nest in the weed patch close beside the Crooked Little Path, chuckling to herself as she listened to Bob's voice. You see, she knew just what he was doing.

It was the same way with Jimmy Skunk and Granny Fox and even Peter Rabbit. All of them hunted and hunted for that nest and watched Bob White and were sure that they knew just where to look for his home, and afterward wondered why it was that they couldn't find it. Jimmy Skunk wanted some of those eggs. Reddy and Granny Fox wanted to catch Mrs. Bob or be ready to gobble up the babies when they should hatch out of those beautiful white eggs. As for Peter Rabbit, he wanted to know where that nest was just out of curiosity. He wouldn't have harmed Mrs. Bob or one of those eggs for the world. But Bob knew that if Peter knew where that nest was, he might visit it when someone was watching him, and something dreadful might happen as a result. So he thought it best to fool Peter just as he did the others, and I think it was. Don't you?

IX

Peter Has Hard Work Believing His Own Eyes

When with your eyes you see a thing
Yet can't believe it so,
Pray tell me what you can believe.
I'd really like to know.

THINGS are that way sometimes. They are so surprising that it doesn't seem that they can be true. Just ask Peter Rabbit or little

Mrs. Peter. Either one will tell you that they have had hard work to believe what their eyes saw. You see, it was this way: Peter knew that somewhere near the dear Old Briar-patch was the home of Bob White. Anyway Bob had said that it was near there, and he himself was never very far away. So Peter didn't doubt that Bob had told him the truth. No one would stay around one place day after day in the beautiful spring-time, when everybody was busy housekeeping, unless his home was very near.

But Peter had looked and looked for that home of Bob White's without ever getting so much as a glimpse of it. He had watched Bob White and had visited every place that he saw Bob go to, but Bob had managed to keep his secret and Peter was no wiser than before, though he was thinner from running about so much. Little Mrs. Peter had tried her best to make him see that it was no business of his. You see, she knew just how Mrs. Bob felt about wanting her home a secret, for little Mrs. Peter had had many anxious hours when her own babies were very small.

Finally Peter did give up, but it was because he had looked in every place he could think of and at last had made up his mind that if Bob White really had a nest in the Green Meadows it certainly wasn't near the dear Old Briar-patch. Then one morning a surprising thing happened. Peter was just getting ready to run over to the Laughing Brook when someone right in front of him there in the Old Briar-patch exclaimed:

"Be careful where you step, Peter Rabbit!"

Peter stopped short and looked to see who had spoken. There, under a tangle of brambles, was little Mrs. Bob White. Peter was surprised, for he had not seen her enter the dear Old Briar-patch.

"Oh!" said he. Then he bowed politely. "How do you do, Mrs. Bob White? I'm glad you've decided to make us a call. I hope Bob is very well. I haven't seen him for several days, but I've heard his whistle and it sounds as if he were feeling very fine."

"He is," replied little Mrs. Bob. Then she added anxiously, "Do please be very careful where you step, Peter."

"Why? What's the matter?" asked Peter, looking down at his feet in a puzzled way.

"Please be very careful where you step, Peter"

Just then Mrs. Peter, who had heard them talking, came hurrying up. Mrs. Bob White became more anxious than ever. "Oh, Mrs. Peter, do, do be careful where *you* step!" she cried.

Mrs. Peter looked as puzzled as Peter did. Just then little Mrs. Bob uttered the softest, sweetest little call, and all at once it seemed to Peter and Mrs. Peter as if the brown leaves which carpeted the dear Old Briar-patch suddenly came to life and started to run. Peter's eyes almost popped out of his head, and he rubbed them twice to make sure that he really saw what he thought he saw. What was it? Why, a whole family of the funniest little birds scurrying as fast as their small legs could take them to the shelter of Mrs. Bob's wings!

X

New Tenants for the Briar-Patch

Who proves himself a neighbor kind
Will find content and peace of mind.

ONE, two, three, four — oh dear, they run so fast I can't count them! Aren't they darlings? I'm so glad you brought them over for us to see, Mrs. Bob. How many are there?" cried little Mrs. Peter, as she and Peter watched the tiny little babies of Bob White scamper to the shelter of their mother's wings under the friendly brambles of the dear Old Briar-patch.

"There are fifteen," replied Mrs. Bob White proudly.

"My gracious, what a family!" exclaimed Peter. "I don't see how you keep track of all of them. I should think you would be worried to death."

"They are a great care," confessed little Mrs. Bob White. "That is why I have brought them over to the Old Briar-patch. I hope you and Mrs. Peter will not mind if we live here for a while. Until they can fly, it is the very safest place I know of."

"We'll be tickled to death to have you here," declared Peter. "We don't own the dear Old Briar-patch, though we've lived here so long we almost feel as if it belongs to us. But of course anyone who wants to is free to live here. I don't know of anyone we would rather have here than you and your family. By the way, I don't see how you could travel far with such little babies. May I ask where you came from?"

Little Mrs. Bob's eyes twinkled. "Certainly," she replied. "We haven't traveled far. We came straight from our home here."

"But where was your home?" Peter asked the question eagerly, for you remember he had spent a great deal of time trying to find that home of the Bob Whites.

"Just over yonder in that little patch of weeds across the Crooked Little Path. You see, it was very handy to the Old Briar-patch," replied Mrs. Bob.

"What?" Peter fairly shouted. "Do you mean to say that you have been living so near as all that?"

Mrs. Bob nodded. "I surely have," she replied. "I've been right where I could see you every day as I sat on my eggs."

"But how did you dare build in such a dangerous place? Why, Reddy and Granny Fox passed within a few feet of you every day! I never heard of such a crazy thing!" Peter looked as if he didn't believe it even yet.

"It was the safest place on the Green Meadows," retorted Mrs. Bob. "I should think that by this time you would have learned, Peter Rabbit, that the safest place to hide is the place where no one will look. The proof of it is right here in these babies of mine. Aren't they darlings? I sat there day after day and watched you and Reddy and Granny Fox and

Jimmy Skunk hunting for me and had many a good laugh all to myself. I knew that not one of you would dream that I would be so foolishly wise as to build my home where it could be so easily found, and therefore you wouldn't look for it there. And I was right."

Mrs. Peter chuckled. "You were just right, Mrs. Bob," she declared. "It is the smartest thing I ever heard of, my dear. If Peter doesn't feel foolish, he ought to. I told him that it was none of his business where your home was, but he was so curious that he would keep hunting for it. And to think that all the time it was close by! Don't you feel foolish, Peter?"

"Yes, my dear, I certainly do," replied Peter meekly. "But now that I know where it was I am satisfied. And I'm glad that Mrs. Bob has brought her family to live in the dear Old Briar-patch. I think it will be great fun watching those youngsters grow, and I can't help thinking that this is a great deal safer for them than the home they have just left."

"That's why I've brought them here," replied Mrs. Bob. "As long as they were only eggs that was the safest place, but now that they have hatched out and can run about, they wouldn't be safe a minute over there. As it is, I expect it won't be long before they will be wanting to get out in the Great World and then my worries will really begin. Bringing up a large family is a great responsibility."

"It is so," declared Mrs. Peter.

XI

Watch Your Step!

Watch your step! Be sure you know
Exactly what lies just before,
Because if you should careless be
'Tis certain you would step no more.

IT wasn't that way with Peter Rabbit. He wasn't afraid that if he didn't watch out he would step no more, not in the Old Briar-patch anyway, but he was afraid, dreadfully afraid, that one of Bob White's babies might step no more. It seemed to Peter that they were always just underfoot. It made him nervous. Every time he moved, little Mrs. Bob or Mrs. Peter was sure to cry, "Watch your step, Peter!" or "Don't step on one of those darlings!"

So every time he moved, Peter looked sharply to see that there wasn't a tiny brown bird hiding under a brown leaf. You know he wouldn't have stepped on one of them for the world. Really there wasn't half as much danger as their fond mother seemed to think, for little as they were, those Bob White babies were very spry, and very smart too. But you know how it is with mothers; they seem to be always expecting something dreadful will happen to their babies. So twenty times a day Peter would hear that warning, "Watch your step!"

Still, in spite of this, he was glad that the Bob White family had moved over to the dear Old Briar-patch. It gave him a chance to learn more about the ways of Bob White and his children than he could possibly have learned in any other way. You know, Peter is always anxious to learn, especially about other people. It seemed to him that never had he seen babies grow as did the little Bob Whites. They were everywhere. There were fifteen of them, and Peter often wondered how under the sun their mother kept track of all of them. But she did. One thing he noticed, and this was that they obeyed promptly whenever she called to them. If Redtail the Hawk came sailing lazily over the Old Briar-patch, watching with sharp eyes to see if anything was going on down there that he didn't know about, little Mrs. Bob would give a warning, and every one of those youngsters would squat down right where he happened to be and not move until she told him

Red-tail the Hawk came sailing lazily over the Old Briar-patch

he might. So old Redtail never once suspected that the Bob White family was there. When Mrs. Bob called them to her, they came running on the instant. Such obedience was beautiful to see.

Then, when they were all nestled under her wings, she would tell them about the Great World and all the dangers that they would have to watch out for when they were big enough to go out into it, and how each one was to be met. As they ran this way and that way in the Old Briar-patch, they picked up tiny seeds. Peter had not supposed that there were so many seeds as those little Bob Whites found. You know Peter does not eat tiny seeds, and so he never had noticed them before. Mrs. Bob led them about, showing them what seeds were best and what to leave alone. They didn't have to be shown but once. Often they varied their fare by picking tiny insects from the low-hanging leaves, and once in a while there would be a struggle between two or more for possession of a worm. Peter always liked to watch this. It was very funny.

In a few days there were no bugs or worms to be found in the Old Briar-patch, at least not on or near the ground. The Bob White family had eaten *every one.*

"I wish they would live here all the time," declared Mrs. Peter. "I don't like bugs and worms. They give me a crawly feeling every time I see them."

But a growing family must have plenty to eat, and at the end of a week Mrs. Bob led her youngsters forth to hunt bugs and worms and seeds on the Green Meadows, but never very far from the Old Briar-patch, so that in case of need they could run back to its friendly shelter. And every night she brought them back there to sleep under the friendly brambles. So after all, it was only for a little while that Peter had to watch his steps, and he was really sorry when he no longer heard that warning every time he moved. You see, he had grown very fond of the little Bob Whites.

XII

The Little Bob Whites at School

Everybody goes to school;
That's the universal rule.
Mother Nature long ago
Said it always should be so.

OF course there are all kinds of schools, but to one kind or another everybody has to go. A lot of people don't know they are going to school, but they are, just the same. If you should ask them what school they go to, they would tell you they don't go to any. But they do just the same. They go to the hardest school of all, the school of experience. That is the school in which we all learn how to live and take care of ourselves. It is just the same with the little meadow and forest people. The four babies of Johnny and Polly Chuck went to school in the Old Orchard just as soon as they were big enough to run around. It was the same way with the children of Peter Rabbit in the dear Old Briar-patch, and the youngsters of Danny and Nanny Meadow

Mouse on the Green Meadows, and Unc' Billy Possum's lively family in the Green Forest, and little Joe Otter's two hopefuls in the Laughing Brook. So of course all the little Bob Whites started in to go to school almost as soon as they were out of their shells.

The very first thing they learned was to mind their parents, which is the very first lesson all little folks must learn. "You see, my dears," explained Mrs. Bob, as they nestled under her wings, "the Great World is full of dangers, especially for little Bob Whites, and so if you want to live to grow up to be as handsome and smart as your father, you must mind instantly when we speak to you."

So as every one of the fifteen little Bob Whites wanted to live to grow up to be as handsome and smart as their father, each one took the greatest care to mind the very second Bob or Mrs. Bob spoke. While they were in the dear Old Briar-patch they were quite safe, but just the same, every little while Mrs. Bob would give the danger signal, which meant to squat and keep perfectly still, or another call that meant to come running to her as fast as ever they could. It wasn't until she was sure that they had learned to mind instantly that she led them out on to the Green Meadows among the grasses and the weeds.

Then there was always real danger as she took great pains to tell them. There was danger from the air where old Redtail the Hawk sailed round and round, watching below for heedless and careless little folks. There was danger from Reddy and Granny Fox and Old Man Coyote, prowling about with sharp eyes and keen ears and wonderful noses, all the time hunting for heedless little people. And there was danger from Mr. Blacksnake and his cousins, slipping silently through the grass.

So the little Bob Whites learned to be always on the watch as they ran this way and that way, hunting for bugs and worms and seeds. At the least little unknown sound they squatted and waited for Mrs. Bob's signal that all was well. She taught them to know Ol' Mistah Buzzard, who wouldn't hurt a feather of them, from old Redtail the Hawk by the way he sailed and sailed without flapping his wings. Just as soon as they could fly a little, she taught them to make sure just where the nearest bushes or trees were so that they could fly to them in case of

Ol' Mistah Buzzard wouldn't hurt the little Bob Whites

sudden danger on the ground. She taught them how to find the safest places in which to spend the night. Oh, there was a great deal for those little Bob Whites to learn! Yes, indeed. And it didn't do to forget a single thing. Forgetting just once might mean a dreadful thing. So they didn't forget. Bob White himself taught them many things, for Bob is wise in the ways of the Great World, and he is the best of fathers. So the little Bob Whites grew and grew until they were too big to nestle under the wings of Mrs. Bob and could fly on swift strong wings. And all the time they were at school without knowing it.

XIII

Farmer Brown's Boy Becomes Thoughtful

For everything that happens
You've but to look to find
There's bound to be a reason;
So keep that fact in mind.

SON," said Farmer Brown one morning at the breakfast table, "we've got the finest looking garden anywhere around. I don't remember ever having a garden with so little harm done by bugs and worms. All our neighbors are complaining that bugs and worms are the worst ever this year, and that their gardens are being eaten up in spite of all that they can do. I'm proud of the way in which you've taken care of ours."

Farmer Brown's boy flushed with pleasure. He had worked hard in that garden ever since the seeds were planted. He had fought the weeds and the bugs and worms. But so had some of his neighbors. Yet in spite of this their gardens were nearly ruined. They had worked just as hard as he had, but the worms and the bugs had been too much for them. He couldn't understand why he had succeeded when they had failed. There must be a reason. There is a reason for everything.

After breakfast he put on his old straw hat and started down to the garden to look it over, still puzzling over the reason why his garden was so much better than others. Just on the edge of the garden was an old board. He lifted one end of it and peeped under. Old Mr. Toad looked up at him and blinked sleepily, but in the most friendly way. Mr. Toad's waistcoat was filled out until it looked too tight for comfort. Farmer Brown's boy smiled as he put the board down gently. He knew what made that waistcoat so tight; it was filled with bugs and worms. "There's a part of the reason," muttered Farmer Brown's boy.

A little farther on he discovered Little Friend the Song Sparrow very busy among the berry bushes. "There's another part of the reason," chuckled Farmer Brown's boy. At the end of a long row he sat down to think it over. There was no doubt that he owed a great deal to Old Mr. Toad and Little Friend and a lot of the feathered folk of the Old Orchard for his fine-looking garden, but he had had their help in other years when his garden had not looked half as well, and yet when there had not been nearly as many bugs and worms as this year. Their help and his own hard work accounted for part of the reason for his fine-looking garden, but he couldn't help feeling that there must be something else he didn't know about.

He was thinking so hard that he sat perfectly still. Presently a pair of bright eyes peeped out at him from under a berry bush. Then right out in front of him stepped a smart, trim little fellow dressed in brown, gray, and white with black trimmings. It was Bob White. He called softly and out ran Mrs. Bob and fifteen children! At a word from Bob they scattered and went to work among the plants.

Farmer Brown's boy held his breath as he watched. They didn't pay the least attention to him because, you know, he sat perfectly still. Some scratched the ground just like the hens at home, and then picked up things so small that he couldn't see what they were. But he knew. He knew that they were tiny seeds. And because all the seeds which he and Farmer Brown had planted were now great strong plants, he knew that these were seeds of weeds.

Bob himself was very busy among the potato vines. He was near enough for Farmer Brown's boy to see what he was doing. He was eating those striped beetles which Farmer Brown's boy had fought so long and which he had come to hate. "One, two, three, four, five, six, seven, eight, nine, ten, eleven," counted Farmer Brown's boy, and then Bob moved on to where he couldn't be seen. Among the squash vines he could see Mrs. Bob, and she was picking off bugs as fast as Bob was taking the potato beetles. What the others were doing he didn't know, but he could guess.

"There's the rest of the reason!" he suddenly exclaimed in triumph. He spoke aloud, and in a twinkling there wasn't a Bob White to be seen.

XIV

A Little Lesson in Arithmetic

Don't say you "hate" arithmetic,
And find it dull and dry.
You'll find it most astonishing
If you sincerely try.

FARMER BROWN'S boy used to feel that way, but he doesn't any more. He never could see any use in puzzling over sums in school. He said that there wasn't anything interesting in it; nothing but hard work. He used to complain about it at home. Farmer Brown would listen awhile, then he would say, "If you live long enough, my son, you will find that figures talk and that they tell the most wonderful things." There was always a twinkle in his eyes when he said this.

Now of course Farmer Brown's boy knew that his father didn't mean that figures could speak right out. Of course not. But he never could understand just what he did mean, and he wasn't interested enough to try to find out. So he would continue to scowl over his arithmetic and wish the teacher wouldn't give such hard lessons. And when the long summer vacation began, he just forgot all about figures and sums until after he discovered Bob White and his family helping to rid the garden of bugs and worms and seeds of weeds.

After he discovered them, he went down to the garden every day to watch them. They soon found out that he wouldn't hurt them, and after that they just paid no attention to him at all, but went right on with their business all about him, and that business was the filling of their stomachs with seeds and worms and bugs. One day Bob White ate twelve caterpillars while Farmer Brown's boy was watching him. He got out a stubby pencil and a scrap of paper.

"If every one of these Bob Whites eats twelve of those horrid worms at one meal that would be — let me see." He wrinkled his brows. "There are Bob and Mrs. Bob and fifteen young Bobs and that makes seventeen. Now if each eats twelve, that will make twelve times seventeen." He put down the figures on his bit of paper and worked over them for a few minutes. "That makes 204 caterpillars for one meal," he muttered, "and in one month of thirty days they would eat 6120 if they only ate one meal a day. But they eat ever so many meals a day and that means—" He stopped to stare at the figures on the bit of paper with eyes round with wonder. Then he whistled a little low whistle of sheer astonishment. "No wonder I've got a good garden when those fellows are at work in it!" he exclaimed.

Then he sat down to watch Mrs. Bob catching cabbage butterflies which he knew were laying the eggs which would hatch out into the worms that spoiled the cabbages. He counted the number she caught while she was in sight. He did the

He counted the number of butterflies
Mrs. Bob caught

same thing with another of the Bob Whites who was catching cucumber beetles, and with another who was hunting grasshoppers. Then he did some more figuring on that bit of paper. When he had finished he got up and went straight down to the cornfield where Farmer Brown was at work.

"I know now what you meant when you used to tell me that figures talk," said he. "Why, they've told me more than I ever dreamed! They've told me that the Bob Whites are the best friends we've got, and that the reason that we've got the best garden anywhere around is just because they have made it so. Why, those little brown birds are actually making money for us, and we never guessed it!"

XV

Farmer Brown's Boy Grows Indignant

TO be indignant is to be angry in a good cause. If you lose your temper and give way to anger because things do not suit you, you are not indignant; you are simply angry. But if anger wells up in your heart because of harm or injustice which is done to someone else, or even to yourself, then you become indignant.

Farmer Brown's boy had spent all his spare time down in the garden watching Bob White and his family. In fact, he had been there so much that all the Bob Whites had come to look on him as harmless if not actually a friend. They just didn't pay him any attention at all, but went about their business as if he were nowhere about. And their business was ridding that garden of bugs and worms and seeds of weeds in order to fill their stomachs. What tickled Farmer Brown's boy was that the bugs and worms of which they seemed the most fond were the very ones which did the most harm to the growing plants.

Over beyond the garden was a field of wheat. You know from wheat comes the flour of which your bread is made. Now there is a certain little bug called the chinch-bug which is such a hungry rascal that when he and a lot of his kind get into a field of wheat, they often spoil the whole crop. They suck the juices from the plants so that they wilt and die. Farmer Brown's boy had heard his neighbors complaining that chinch-bugs were very bad that year, and he knew that they must be by the looks of the wheat on the farms of his neighbors. But Farmer Brown's wheat looked as fine as wheat could look. It was very plain that there were no chinch-bugs there, and he often had wondered why, when they were so bad in the fields of his neighbors.

Farmer Brown's boy noticed that Bob White and his family spent a great deal of time in the wheat field. One day he noticed Bob picking something from a stem of wheat. He went over to see what it might be. Of course Bob scurried away, but when Farmer Brown's boy looked at that wheat plant he found some chinch-bugs on it. Then he knew what Bob had been doing. He had been picking off and eating those dreadful little bugs. And he knew, too, why it was that their wheat field was the best for miles around. It was because Bob White and his family hunted for and ate those bugs as fast as they appeared.

"Hurrah for you! You're the greatest little helpers a farmer ever had!" cried Farmer Brown's boy, and hurried off to tell Farmer Brown what he had found out.

So the summer passed, and the cool crisp days of autumn came. The wheat had been harvested and the vegetables gathered and stored away. Jack Frost had begun to paint the maple trees red and yellow, the garden was bare, and the stubble in the wheat field a golden brown. The little feathered people who do not like cold weather had flown away to the sunny Southland, led by Ol' Mistah Buzzard. Striped Chipmunk, Chatterer the Red Squirrel, and Happy Jack the Gray Squirrel were busy from morning till night storing away seeds and nuts on which to live through the long, cold winter. These were glorious days, and Bob White loved every one of them.

"Son," said Farmer Brown one

They were busy storing away seeds and nuts

morning, "those Bob Whites must be fat with the good living they have had. Seeing that we have fed them off the farm all summer, don't you think that it is their turn to feed us? I think broiled Bob White on toast would taste pretty good. The shooting season begins next week, so I suppose you will get out your gun and shoot a few of those Bob Whites for us." There was a twinkle, a kindly twinkle, in his eyes as he spoke.

But Farmer Brown's boy didn't see that twinkle. His face grew red. A hot anger filled his heart. He was indignant. He was very indignant to think that his father should ever hint at such a thing. But he didn't forget to be respectful.

"No, sir!" said he. "I wouldn't shoot one of them for anything in the world! They don't owe us anything; we owe them. If it hadn't been for them, we wouldn't have had half a crop of wheat, and our garden would have been just as poor as those of our neighbors. I'm not going to shoot 'em, and I'm not going to let anyone else shoot 'em if I can help it, so there!"

XVI

Farmer Brown's Boy Talks Things Over

There's nothing to compare with love
In earth or sea or up above.

IF love prevailed everywhere there would be no terrible wars, no prisons, no dreadful poverty, no bitter quarrels between those who work and those for whom they work. And on the Green Meadows and in the Green Forest there would be no fear of man and no frightful suffering from traps and terrible guns. Love, that wonderful great thing which is contained in one little word of four letters, could and would bring joy and happiness to every heart for all time if only we would give it a chance.

It was love in the heart of Farmer Brown's boy which made him indignant when Farmer Brown hinted that he might take his gun and shoot Bob White and his family. You see, he had made friends with the Bob Whites and learned to love them, and no one can bear the thought of hurting those they love.

He had replied to his father respectfully, but his face had flushed red and in his voice there had been the ring of indignation, which is a certain kind of anger. Farmer Brown actually chuckled when he heard it. Then he turned and held out his big hand.

"Shake hands, son," said he. "I was just trying you out to see what you would say. You know you used to be very fond of hunting, and I was just wondering if your love of killing, or trying to kill, was stronger than your sense of right and justice. Now I know that it isn't, and I'm ever so glad. So you think the Bob

Whites have earned our protection?"

Farmer Brown's boy's face flushed again, but this time it was with pleasure.

"Oh, Dad, I'm so glad you don't want them killed to eat!" he cried. "I ought to have known that you were just teasing me. I did like to hunt with my gun once, but that was when I didn't know as much as I do now. It was exciting to try to find the birds and then see if I could hit them. I just thought of them as wild things good to eat and so smart that I had to be a little bit smarter to get them. I never thought of them as having any feelings. But now I know that they love, and fear, and suffer pain, and work, and play, and are glad and sad, just like people. I know because I've watched them. So I don't want to hurt them or allow them to be hurt any more than I would real people. Why I *love* 'em! I wouldn't have anything happen to them for the world. I'm dreadfully afraid something will happen to some of them when the hunting season begins. Can't we do anything for them?"

"We can put up some signs warning all hunters to keep off our farm and forbidding all shooting," replied Farmer Brown. "Then if Bob White and his family are smart enough to stay on our land I guess they will be safe, but if they go on the land of other people they are likely to be shot unless—" he paused.

"Unless I can get other people who own land near us to put up signs and keep the hunters off and promise not to shoot the Bob Whites themselves!" exclaimed Farmer Brown's boy eagerly.

Farmer Brown smiled. "Exactly, my son," said he. "It is your chance to get even; to do something for the little friends who have done so much for you. Tomorrow is Saturday, and there will be no school. You may have all day in which to see what you can do with the neighbors to save Bob White and his family from the hunters. Listen! Bob would be a blessing if for nothing but his message of good cheer. But to the cheer he puts into the world is the daily help he gives. The man who kills Bob White kills one of our best friends and helpers, and his shot hurts us more than it does poor little Bob. Now let's go over to the barn and see about making those signs."

XVII

A Beautiful Day Made Dreadful

A pity 'tis, aye, 'tis a shame
That rests on all mankind,
That human beings in cruelty
Can sport and pleasure find.

THERE never was a more beautiful day than that crisp October one. It was one of those days when you just feel all over how good it is to be alive. Bob White felt it. He

Bob tingled with the joy of living

tingled all over with the joy of living just as soon as he opened his eyes very early that morning. He whistled for very joy. He loved all the Great World, and he felt that all the Great World loved him. He wanted to tell the Great World so. The Merry Little Breezes of Old Mother West Wind, tumbling out of the big bag in which she had brought them down from the Purple Hills to play all day long on the Green Meadows, danced over to tell him that they loved him. This made Bob still happier.

A certain man tramping along the road toward the home of Farmer

Jones was feeling glad, but his gladness was of a different kind. "I guess we are going to have some sport, old fellow," said he to the dog trotting at his heels, and shifted a terrible gun from one shoulder to the other.

Now if Bob White had understood the warning given him by Farmer Brown's boy he never, never would have done as he did. But he didn't understand that warning, and so when he took it into his pretty little head that he wanted to try his wings he led his family straight over to the land of Farmer Jones. He often had been there before, and he saw no reason why he shouldn't go there as often as he pleased. No harm had come from these previous visits. So straight over to the stubble of Farmer Jones' wheat field he led the way, and soon he and his family were very busy picking up scattered grains of wheat and were happy as you or I would be over a good breakfast.

Right in the midst of it Bob's quick ears heard footsteps. He stretched his neck to peep over the stubble, and suddenly all the gladness and brightness of the day were blotted out. What he saw was a dog with his nose to the ground and he was following the scent that one of

Bob's children made as he ran about picking up wheat. Suddenly the dog stopped and stood perfectly still, with one foreleg and nose pointing straight at a certain spot. Bob knew that right at that spot one of his children was squatting close to the ground. As still as a statue stood the dog. From behind him came a man walking slowly and carefully and with a terrible gun held in readiness. When he reached the dog he sent him on. There was nothing for the Bob White squatting there to do but fly. Up into the air he shot on swift wings.

"Bang!" went the terrible gun,

and down dropped that little brown bird. At the sound of the terrible gun up jumped all the rest of Bob White's children in terrible fright, for never before had they heard such a dreadful noise. "Bang!" went the gun again, but this time only a few brown feathers floated to the ground. Bob and Mrs. Bob waited until after the second bang before they too took to the air, for they had had experience and knew that after the second bang they were likely to be safe for a while.

The Bob Whites had scattered in all directions as they had been taught to do when in danger. Bob flew straight over to Farmer Brown's wheat field, and there presently he began to call. One after another of his family answered, all but the one who had fallen at the first shot.

"Got one, anyway," said the hunter, as he loaded his terrible gun, and actually looked happy as he went over to help his dog hunt for the Bob White who had fallen at the first terrible bang.

XVIII

The Disappointed Hunter

It never does to count upon
A thing until you're sure.
It's often less than you expect,
But very seldom more.

THE hunter who had shot one of Bob White's children chuckled gleefully as he went forward to pick up the poor little brown bird. He was having what he called sport. It never entered his head to think of how the Bob Whites must feel. He probably didn't think that they had any feelings. He was pleased that he had made a successful shot, and he was pleased to think that he was to have that little brown bird to eat, though of course he didn't need it the least bit in the world, having plenty of other things to eat.

But when he reached the place where he had seen the little Bob White fall, there was no little brown bird there. No, sir, there was not a sign of that little bird save a few feathers. You see, he hadn't killed the little Bob White as he had supposed, but had broken a wing so that it could not fly. But there was nothing the matter with its legs, and no sooner had it hit the ground than it had run as fast as ever it could through the stubble. So the little Bob White wasn't where the hunter was looking for it at all.

Of course his dog helped him hunt, and with that wonderful nose of his he soon found the scent of that little Bob White and eagerly followed it. It just happened that in that field near where the little Bob White fell was an old home of Johnny Chuck, and all around the entrance to it the sand had been spread out. Now sand does not hold scent. The little Bob White knew nothing about that, for he had not lived long enough to learn all that a Bob White has to learn, but he did see the open doorway. Across the yellow sand he ran and into the doorway and just a little way down the hall, where he hid under some dry, brown leaves which had blown in there. He was almost the color of them himself as he squatted close to the ground and drew his feathers as close to his body as possible. In doing this he was doing a very wise thing, though he didn't know it at the time. You see, his feathers drawn tightly against his body that way prevented the scent which might have told the keen nose of that dog where he was.

As it was, the dog lost the scent at the edge of the sand, and neither he nor the hunter once thought to look in that old hole. So while they hunted and hunted, the little Bob White squatted perfectly still, though his broken wing hurt him dreadfully, and the ache of it made his eyes fill with tears. At last the hunter gave up the search. He was too impatient to kill more.

"Must be I just wounded him," said he, without one thought of how dreadful it must be to be wounded. "Probably a fox will get him."

With that he sent his dog on to try to find the little Bob White's brothers and sisters, his terrible gun held ready to shoot the instant he should see one of them. He was having great sport, was that hunter, while in the hall of Johnny Chuck's old house lay a little brown Bob White faint with suffering and dreadful fright. It would have been bad enough to simply have such a fright, but to have a broken wing and because of this to feel quite helpless — well, can you imagine anything worse?

XIX

Frightened, Wounded, and Alone

Oh, cruel is the thoughtless deed
That wounds another without need.

SQUATTING under the brown, dead leaves which had blown into the doorway of the old house made long ago in the wheat field of Farmer Jones by Johnny Chuck was that poor little Bob White. Tears filled his eyes, tears of fright and

Tears filled the poor little Bob White's eyes

pain. He tried to wink them back and to think what he should do next, but he was too bewildered to think. To be bewildered is to be so upset that you cannot understand what has happened or is happening. It was just so with this little Bob White.

With his brothers and sisters he had been happily picking up his breakfast that beautiful October morning. Without the least warning a great dog had threatened to catch him, and he had taken to his swift, strong, little wings. As he did so he had seen a great two-legged creature pointing a stick at him, but he had not feared. All summer long he had seen two-legged creatures like this one, and they had not harmed him. Indeed, he had come to look on them as his friends, for had not Farmer Brown's boy watched him and his brothers and sisters day after day, and not once offered even to frighten them? So he had had no fear of this one.

Then from the end of that stick pointed at him had leaped fire and smoke, and there had been a terrible noise. Something had struck him, something that stung, and burned and tore his tender flesh, and one of his swift, strong little wings had become useless, so that he fell heavily to the ground. Then he had run swiftly until he found this hiding place, and, with his little heart going pit-a-pat, pit-a-pat with terror, had squatted close under the friendly brown leaves while the great dog and the two-legged creature had looked for him. Now they had given him up and gone away. At least, he could not hear them.

What did it all mean? Why had this dreadful thing happened to him? What had he done that the two-legged creature should try to kill him with the terrible fire-stick? Outside the day was as beautiful as ever, but all the joy of it was gone. Instead, it was filled with terror. What should he do now? What *could* he do? Where were his father and mother and brothers and sisters? Were such dreadful things happening to them as had happened to him? Would he ever see them again?

Presently he heard a faraway whistle, a sad, anxious whistle. It was the whistle of his father, Bob White. He was calling his family together. Then he heard answering whistles, and he knew that the others were safe and would soon join Bob White. But he did not dare answer himself. He crawled to the doorway and peeped out. He could see the great dog and the cruel two-legged creature with the terrible fire-stick far away on the other side of the field. He tried to leap into the air and fly as he had been used to doing, but only flopped helplessly. One wing was useless and dragged on the ground. It hurt so that the pain made him faint.

He closed his eyes and lay still for a few minutes, panting. Then a new thought filled him with another terrible fear. If Reddy Fox or Old Man Coyote or Redtail the Hawk should happen along, how could he escape without the use of his wings? If only he were not alone! If only he could reach his father and mother perhaps they could help him. He struggled to his feet and began to walk towards that distant whistle. It was slow work. He was weak and faint, and the drooping wing dragged through the stiff stubble and hurt so that it seemed as if he could not stand it. Often he squatted down and panted with weariness and pain and fright. Then he would go on again. He was terribly thirsty, but there was no water to drink. So at last he crawled under a fence, and then suddenly, right in front of him, was one of those two-legged creatures! Right then and there the little Bob White gave up all hope.

XX

Farmer Brown's Boy Speaks His Mind

You cannot always surely tell
If things be ill or things be well.

WHEN the poor, suffering, wounded little Bob White crawled under the fence he didn't know it, but he had crawled onto the land of Farmer Brown, where a sign warned all hunters to keep off—

that no shooting would be allowed there. And when he looked up and saw right in front of him one of those two-legged creatures like the one with the terrible fire-stick, and at once had given up all hope, he had been too sick at heart and suffering too much to recognize Farmer Brown's boy.

But that is just who it was. You see, Farmer Brown's boy had been so anxious for fear that some hunter would come over on his father's land in spite of the signs, that he had gone down on the Green Meadows just as soon as he had eaten his breakfast. He had seen the hunter on the land of Farmer Jones and had heard him shoot. With all his heart Farmer Brown's boy had hoped that the hunter had missed. Now as he looked down and saw the poor little suffering bird he knew that the hunter had not missed, and fierce anger swelled his heart. He quite forgot that he himself used to hunt with a terrible gun before he had learned to love the little people of the Green Meadows, the Green Forest, and the Old Pasture.

He stooped and very tenderly lifted the little Bob White, who closed his eyes and was sure that now all would soon be over.

"You poor little thing! You poor, poor little thing!" said Farmer Brown's boy as he looked at the torn and broken wing. Then he looked across at the hunter and scowled savagely. Just then the hunter saw him and at once started toward him. You see, the hunter thought that perhaps if he offered Farmer Brown's boy money he would allow him to hunt on Farmer Brown's land. He knew that was where Bob White and all his family had flown to. When he reached the fence, he saw the little Bob White in the hands of Farmer Brown's boy.

"Hello!" exclaimed the hunter in

"You poor, poor little thing!"

surprise, "I guess that's my bird!"

"I guess it's nothing of the sort!" retorted Farmer Brown's boy.

"Oh, yes, it is," replied the hunter. "I shot it a little while ago, but it got away from me. I'll thank you to hand it over to me, young man."

"I'll do nothing of the sort," retorted Farmer Brown's boy. "It may be the bird you shot, more shame to you, but it isn't yours; it's mine. I found it on our land, and it belongs to me if it belongs to anyone."

Now the hunter was tempted to reply sharply, but remembering that he wanted to get this boy's permission to hunt on Farmer Brown's land, he bit the angry reply off short and said instead, "Why don't you wring its neck? If you'll get your father to let me shoot on your land, I'll kill another for you, and then you will have a fine dinner."

Farmer Brown's boy grew red in the face. "Don't you dare put your foot on this side of the fence!" he cried. "I'll have you know that these Bob Whites are my very best friends. They've worked for me all summer long, and do you suppose I'm going to let any harm come to them now if I can help it? Not much! Look how this poor little thing is suffering.

And you call it sport. Bah! The law lets you hunt them, but it's a bad law. It's a horrid law. If they did any harm it would be different. But instead of doing harm they work for us all summer long, and then when the crops which they have helped us save are harvested, we turn around and allow them to be shot! But they can't be shot on this land, and the sooner you get away the better I'll like it."

Instead of getting angry the hunter laughed good-naturedly. "All right, I'll keep off your land, sonny," said he. "But you needn't get so excited. They're only birds, and were made to be shot."

"No more than you were!" retorted Farmer Brown's boy. "And they've got feelings just as you have. This poor little thing is trembling like a leaf in my hand. I'm not going to wring its neck. I'm going to try to cure it." With this Farmer Brown's boy turned his back on the hunter and started for home. And the poor little Bob White, not understanding, had no more hope than before.

XXI

What Happened to the Little Bob White

WITH his eyes tightly closed because of the terror in his heart, the little Bob White was being carried by Farmer Brown's boy. Very tender was the way in which he was handled, and after a while he began to take a little comfort in the warmth of the hand which held him. Once in a while Farmer Brown's boy would gently smooth the feathers of the little head and say, "Poor little chap."

Straight home went Farmer Brown's boy. Very, very gently he bathed the wounds of the little Bob White. Then, as gently as he could, he put the broken bones of the wing back in place and bound them there with little strips of thin wood to keep them from slipping. It hurt dreadfully, and the little Bob White didn't know what it all meant. But he had suffered so much already that a little more suffering didn't matter much, and he didn't so much as peep.

When it was all over he was put into a box with a bed of soft, clean hay, a little dish of water which he could reach by just stretching out his head, and a handful of wheat, and then he was left alone. He was too sick and weary to want to do anything but squat down in that bed of hay and rest. He was still afraid of what might happen to him, but it was not such a great fear as before, for there had been something comforting in the gentle touch of Farmer Brown's boy. He didn't understand at all what those strange wrappings about his body meant, but a lot of the ache and pain had gone from the broken wing.

So he drank gratefully of the water, for he had been burning with thirst, and then settled himself as comfortably as possible and in no time at all was asleep. Yes, sir, he was asleep! You see, he was so worn out with fright and pain that he couldn't keep his eyes open. Ever so many times during the day Farmer Brown's boy came to see how he was getting along, and was so very gentle and whistled to him so softly that his little heart no longer went pit-a-pat with fear.

The next morning the little Bob White felt so much better that he was up bright and early and made a good breakfast of the wheat left for him. But it seemed very queer not to be able to move his wings. He couldn't lift them even the teeniest, weeniest bit because, you see, Farmer Brown's boy had bound them to his sides with strips of cloth so that he couldn't even try to fly. This was so that that broken wing might get well and strong again.

Now of course the little Bob White had lived out of doors all his life, and Farmer Brown's boy knew that he never could be quite happy in the house. So he made a wire pen in the henyard, and in one end he made the nicest little shelter of pine boughs under which the little Bob White could hide. He put a little dish of clean water in the pen and scattered wheat on the ground, and then he put the little Bob White in there.

As soon as he was left quite alone the little Bob White ran all about to see what his new home was like. You see, there was nothing the matter with his legs.

"I can't get out," thought he, when he had been all around the pen, "but neither can anyone get in, so I am safe and that is something to be thankful for. This two-legged creature is not at all like the one with the terrible fire-stick, and I am beginning to like him. I haven't got to fear Reddy Fox or Old Man Coyote or Redtail the Hawk. I guess that really I am a lot better off than if I were out on the Green Meadows unable to fly. Perhaps, when my wing gets well, I will be allowed to go. I wonder where my father and mother and brothers and sisters are and if any of them were hurt by that terrible fire-stick."

XXII

A Joyous Day for the Bob Whites

Thrice blessed be the girl or boy
Who fills another's heart with joy.

ONE day just by chance Bob White flew up in a tree where he could look down in Farmer Brown's henyard, and there he discovered the lost little Bob and talked with him. Then Bob White

He could look down in Farmer Brown's henyard

flew back to the Green Meadows where little Mrs. Bob was anxiously waiting for him, and his heart was light. Mrs. Bob was watching for him and flew to meet him.

"It's all right!" cried Bob. "I found him over in Farmer Brown's henyard." Of course "him" meant the young Bob White who had been given up as killed.

"What?" exclaimed Mrs. Bob. "What is a henyard, and what is he doing there?"

"A henyard is a place where Farmer Brown keeps a lot of big, foolish birds," explained Bob, "and little Bob is a prisoner there."

"How dreadful!" cried Mrs. Bob. "If he's a prisoner, how can you say it's all right?"

"Because it is," replied Bob. "He's perfectly safe there, and he wouldn't be if he were here with us. You see, he can't fly. One of his wings was broken by the shot from that terrible gun. Farmer Brown's boy found him and has been very kind to him. He fixed that wing so that I believe it is going to get quite as well as ever. You know quite as well as I do how much chance little Bob would have had over here with a broken wing. Reddy Fox or Redtail the Hawk or someone else would have been sure to get him sooner or later. But up there they can't, because he is in a wire pen. He can't get out, but neither can they get in, and so he is safe. He and Farmer Brown's boy are great friends. With my own eyes I saw him feed from the hand of Farmer Brown's boy. Do you know, I believe that boy is truly our friend and can be trusted."

"That is what Peter Rabbit is always saying, but after all we've suffered from them, I can't quite make up my mind that any of those great two-legged creatures are to be trusted," said little Mrs. Bob. "I've got to see for myself."

"You shall," declared Bob. "To-morrow morning you shall go up there and I'll stay here to look after the rest of the youngsters. I am afraid if we left them alone some of them would be careless or foolish enough to go where the hunters with terrible guns would find them."

So the next morning Mrs. Bob went up to visit young Bob, and she saw all that Bob had seen the day before. She returned with a great load off her mind. She knew that Bob was right, and that Farmer Brown's boy had proved himself a true friend from whom there was nothing to fear. The next day Bob and Mrs. Bob took the whole family up there, for Farmer Brown's boy had scattered food for them just outside the henyard where the biddies could not get it, and Bob was smart enough to know that no hunters would dare look for them so close to Farmer Brown's house. Morning after morning they went up there to get their breakfast, and they didn't even fly when Farmer Brown's boy and Farmer Brown himself came out to watch them eat.

Then one morning a wonderful thing happened. Farmer Brown's boy took young Bob out of his pen in the henyard. Young Bob looked quite himself by this time, for the strips of cloth which had bound his broken wing in place had been taken off, and his wing was as good as ever. Farmer Brown's boy took him outside the henyard and gently put him down on the ground.

"There you are! Now go and join your family and in the future keep out of the way of hunters," said he, and laughed to see young Bob scamper over to join his brothers and sisters.

Such a fuss as they made over him! Suddenly Bob White flew up to the top of a post, threw back his head and whistled with all his might, "Bob White! Bob White! Bob White!" You see, he just had to tell all the Great World of the joy in his heart, although this was not the time of year in which he usually whistles.

And this is how it happened that Bob White and his whole family came regularly to Farmer Brown's for their breakfasts, and no hunter ever had another chance to carry fright and suffering and sorrow into their midst.

So this is all about Bob White and his family, because Ol' Mistah Buzzard has come all the way up from Ol' Virginny for me to tell you about him and his adventures. I've promised to do it in the very next book.

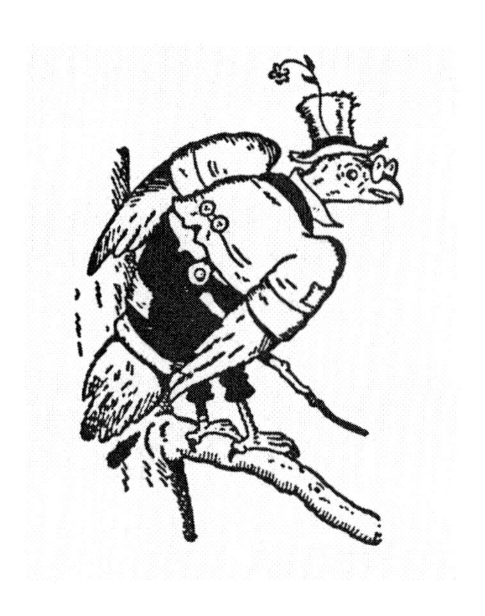